BANK SHOT

Valerie Pankratz Froese

BANK SHOT

Valerie Pankratz Froese

James Lorimer & Company Ltd., Publishers
Toronto

James Lorimer & Company Ltd., Publishers acknowledges funding support from
the Ontario Arts Council (OAC), an agency of the Government of Ontario.
We acknowledge the support of the Canada Council for the Arts, which
last year invested $153 million to bring the arts to Canadians throughout the
country. This project has been made possible in part by the Government of
Canada and with the support of Ontario Creates.

Cover design: Tyler Cleroux
Cover image: Shutterstock

Library and Archives Canada Cataloguing in Publication (Paperback)

Title: Bank shot / Valerie Pankratz Froese.
Names: Pankratz Froese, Valerie, author.
Series: Sports stories.
Description: Series statement: Sports stories
Identifiers: Canadiana (print) 20210202394 | Canadiana (ebook) 20210202424
    | ISBN 9781459416390 (softcover) | ISBN 9781459416406 (EPUB)
Classification: LCC PS8631.A555 B46 2021 | DDC jC813/.6—dc23

Published by:	Distributed in Canada by:	Distributed in the US by:
James Lorimer & Company Ltd., Publishers 117 Peter Street, Suite 304 Toronto, ON, Canada M5V 0M3 www.lorimer.ca	Formac Lorimer Books 5502 Atlantic Street Halifax, NS, Canada B3H 1G4	Lerner Publisher Services 241 1st Ave. N. Minneapolis, MN, USA 55401 www.lernerbooks.com

Printed and bound in Canada.
Manufactured by Friesens Corporation in Altona, Manitoba,
Canada in June 2021.
Job #277239

Dedicated to John Matthews, a teacher ahead of his time.

Contents

1 Outside MY LITTLE WORLD

"C'mon, go hard. You're almost done!" Coach A encouraged as we finished the last set of lines.

I reached the end, along with my best friend, Hala. With my hands on my knees, I bent over and breathed hard. It was done. The last tryout for the grade eight girls' basketball team was finished. I had given my best. Now the wait to see who made the team would feel like forever.

"Great job, girls," Coach A said as the last group finished up. "Bring it in."

We gathered around Coach, most of us still panting. Coach A had worked us hard today. I think she wanted to see who was willing to push themselves and who could dig down deep. With twenty girls trying out, she had to find a way to make cuts.

"I want to thank all of you for coming out on your lunch hour to try out for the team. I wish I could keep all of you, but I can't. The list will be up tomorrow at noon and practices will start the following day."

Hala and I looked at each other and smiled. We were both excited about playing together. Hala had played the year before. She would make the team for sure. I hadn't tried out the year before and really was not very good at all. When I'd wanted to try out in grade seven, mom had told me that my family duty came first and she needed me to look after my little brother, Rory. When I had tried to ask again, she put her hand up like a stop sign. The discussion was over just like that. Now, in grade eight, I had tried out without telling her.

We all rushed into the change room and quickly got ready to head back to afternoon class.

"I can't wait until tomorrow," Jenna said. "Why can't she just tell us now?"

"I know," Rachel added. "It's torture!"

We all laughed in agreement. As we left the gym, Jenna swatted me playfully with her gym bag.

"You did good, Jo," she said.

"Thanks, Jenna," I replied.

I smiled as I walked down the hall. The routine of tryouts and the fun with the girls had been great. It was new to me to be a part of something outside my world of studying and taking care of Rory.

Not everyone could handle my little brother. He was not good with new people. After one of the babysitters had grabbed his arm and left a bruise, Mom would not leave him with anyone but me. Lucky me.

I loved Rory, but with Mom starting work early and getting home late, I wasn't free to do any of the extra school clubs. That's just how it was.

Hala had begged me to try out for the team, even when I said I couldn't. Finally, I had given in. Lunch hours I could do. I thought it would be fun. I didn't think I would make the team, so then at least I could tell Hala I had tried. I hadn't counted on the feelings I had, working hard and getting to know the girls. Now, I wanted more than anything to make the team. But I had no idea what I was going to do if I did.

2 The LIST

The next day Hala found me by my locker as soon as the school lunch bell rang.

"Let's go," she urged. "Coach A said the team list would be up at noon."

I didn't know what Hala was so worried about. Everyone knew she would be the first choice for the school basketball team.

"Okay," I said. I closed my science textbook and stuffed it in my backpack. "I'm coming."

"I am so nervous," Hala said.

"You are the best player, Hala! Relax."

When we entered the gym, a few girls were already standing in front of the list Coach A had taped to the wall. Emma was running her finger down the list, looking for her name. I saw her finger move from the bottom of the list, then back up to the top, and down again. Finally, with her head down, she slowly left the gym. She avoided looking at us as she walked out.

"Poor Emma," I said to Hala. She ran to join the

small group gathered in front of the list.

In seconds there was a big smile on Hala's face. Of course she had made it.

"Congratulations," I said.

I did not think that my name would be on the list, but I had to know for sure.

I felt tears stinging my eyes and everything became blurry. I couldn't even see the names on the list. I stepped back and pretended to be checking my phone for a message.

Hala noticed I had moved away. "Jo, what are you doing? Get over here." Hala turned back to the list and started scanning for my name. "You made it!" She turned and grabbed me with both arms and started jumping up and down. "We're on the team together!"

I couldn't believe it. "What? Where?" Hala pointed about halfway down the list.

I looked where she was pointing. There it was, in big bold letters. Joanna Beck. I had actually made it. A smile covered my entire face, then I saw the note at the bottom of the paper.

Please submit your parent consent forms and fee payment to Coach A at the noon meeting on Friday.

Mom didn't know that I had tried out for the team. When I had tried to bring it up a few weeks before, the hand came up again. She'd told me, "Jo, I need you to take care of Rory for the rest of this school year. After that, we will see. He needs consistency and right now I just don't have time to search for a caretaker that is a good fit for him. I am sorry, but for now the good fit is you."

Now that I had made the team, I really wanted to play. I had to find a way to explain this to my mom.

"Hey, Jo!!" Hala said. "We made it. This is going to be awesome!" Hala was staring at me. "What's wrong with you?"

I nodded. "Nothing. I just can't believe it!" I looked at the clock. "Let's go. We are going to be late for Math."

The rest of the day passed slowly. I was glad that we were working on our own most of the day and that I didn't have to talk to anyone. I couldn't concentrate. I just kept going over how to tell my mom. The first full team practice was the next day and I did not want to miss it.

Finally, the bell sounded to end the school day. I went to get Rory and headed home, as always.

I greeted Mom when she came home from work.

"Hi, Jo." She looked tired. Great.

"What's for dinner, Mom?" Rory shouted. "Can we have noodles?"

All my little brother ever wanted to eat was noodles. He didn't care much what kind — spaghetti, macaroni, linguini, penne, it didn't matter. He just loved pasta, pasta and not much else.

The three of us sat down to eat. Rory went on and

on about a car project he was working on at school. He needed Mom to help him find stuff for the project.

"Mom! I have to bring it to school tomorrow!" he shouted. "I will be the only one with no supplies!"

"I'm sure you won't be the only one," Mom began.

"Yes, I will, Mom. We have to get stuff today."

"Well, I really don't know what we have here. But we can look."

So that's how the evening was spent. Mom and Rory spent the entire night looking through the house for any little thing that Rory could use for his project. Mom was getting stressed as the evening went on and they still didn't have all the stuff he needed.

When they were finally done, I saw Mom go into the living room and put her head in her hands.

"Mom?" I said, as I stepped into the room. "Can I talk to you about something?"

"Jo, I'm sorry. I have a killer headache. Not now."

This was not going to be a good time to tell her about basketball. I realized that there was probably never going to be a good time. Who was I kidding?

"Okay. Night, Mom," I said instead.

"Good night, Jo," she said, still holding her head.

I went to my room, but I couldn't sleep.

3 The Lies BEGIN

When my alarm went off the next morning, I felt groggy. I must have slept a little, but I felt like I was still in a fog. I shuffled out of my room to wake Rory. Mom always left for work early and stayed late. Rory was already up, sorting through the stuff for his car.

"C'mon," I said. "Put that in your backpack and let's have breakfast."

I'd exaggerated when I said Rory only ate noodles. He did eat a few other things. Rice pops cereal was one of them. He ate the same thing every morning. I put some leftover pasta in a container and gave it to him with a juice box to take for lunch.

The twenty-minute walk to school seemed to take even longer than usual. The wind was cold as we trudged through the snow. We were used to the cold. We did this walk every morning and then again after school. But somehow, today felt longer and colder than usual.

We finally got to the playground. I left my brother there to wait for his teacher to call them in. The junior high students were in a different section of the school and it took me a few minutes to walk back to my entrance.

Hala was there already when I arrived. "Hey," she said. "That math homework was ridiculous. Why didn't you answer my text? I needed help."

"Huh? Math homework? I didn't know we had math homework."

"Jo, what is with you? Honestly, ever since yesterday afternoon it's like you are somewhere else."

"Math homework?" I said again. "What did I miss?" I ignored her question.

Hala showed me the assignment. Later, at break time, I pulled out my notebook and got to work.

"Hey, what's the answer for number four?" Hala asked when I was done.

"It's $y=7$." It was an easy question and I had finished the homework quickly without having to use the lunch hour. Math came easy to me. Basketball came easy to Hala. "Here, I'll show you how to do it."

"Forget it, no time." Hala closed her book with a smile. "Let's see if the gym is open. Maybe we can get in some extra shooting practice. We have fifteen minutes left in break."

For a little bit, I had forgotten about basketball. But now it all came back to me.

"Hala," I began, "I'm not feeling great. If I don't feel better by the end of the day, I think I will just go right home after school. Can you tell Coach A?"

"But you were perfectly fine a few minutes ago."

"I know," I said, putting my hand on my head. "I can just feel one of these killer headaches coming on."

"Okay, do you want me to stay with you?"

"No, no, that's okay. You go to the gym. I'll be fine."

Hala looked at me for a moment. I think she was trying to decide what a good friend would do. "Are you sure? I can stay with you if you want."

"I said I'll be fine, really, you go. No sense in both of us missing out."

"Okay, if you're sure you don't mind."

"It's fine, Hala. I just need to take it easy."

That seemed to convince her and she headed toward the gym.

With nothing to distract me, all I could think about was basketball. I thought about not being able to go to practice. I thought about not having my basketball forms signed. And I thought about not having the money to pay the fees.

When the school day finally ended, I left quickly, picked up my brother and headed home. Rory spent the whole time talking about his car, the problems he had and how he had fixed them. It turned out that the teacher had brought in a lot of extra supplies, so Rory didn't have to stress Mom out after all. If we had known, maybe I would have been able to talk to her about basketball.

That night we had — you guessed it — pasta for dinner. Mom and I had a creamy sauce on ours and also some chicken fingers and salad. Rory ate four lettuce leaves, then pounded back the plain pasta.

★★★

Told Coach A u weren't feeling well, Hala texted after dinner.

Thanks, what did she say? I texted back.

Just next time to come and talk to her yourself. But it was fine.

Was she mad?

I don't think so. Remember there is a lunch meeting tomorrow. Coach A wants to talk about what she expects. And don't forget to bring the forms and money.

Oh, ok. Right, tomorrow was Friday.

Practices are going to start half an hour after school. She says she needs a little break from teaching before jumping into coaching. Details tomorrow. R u feeling better? Hala texted.

Ya, I'm fine, I lied. C u tmrw.

What was I supposed to say? Yes? No? Not really? I didn't really even know. I still had a sick feeling in the pit of my stomach, but I didn't think it was anything that staying home was going to cure. I knew I had to deal with this head-on. I had an idea. It was risky, but maybe I could get away with it.

4 THE SECRET

Mom had a jar of emergency money tucked away in the cupboard. It had been there for so long that I knew she didn't remember it. I took my basketball fees from the jar. I planned to pay it back as soon as I could get to the bank, and I knew Mom wouldn't notice.

Then I needed Mom's signature on the forms. I practised signing Mom's name on a blank paper several times before signing the form. Coach A was never going to question that signature. I did a good job.

The lunch meeting started right on schedule. All the girls were dropping off their permission forms on a small desk in front of Coach A. Most of the girls' parents had already sent an e-transfer for the fees, but some girls handed Coach A the cash. I added my signed forms to the top of the pile and gave her my forty dollars.

"Okay, I think we will get started," Coach A began. "I see we are all here, so let's start with what I expect of you. Number one — you must show commitment to this team if you want to play. You will attend all the practices — no excuses unless you are too ill to come to school. Do not plan birthdays and special events on practice days. You have the practice schedule for the whole season. I expect you to work around it. I also expect your full effort at every practice. We have twelve girls on this team. There are more who did not make the team and would be happy to take your place. At practice, we go hard so that we can play hard in the games. You will make every decision based on what is best for the team, not what's best for you. When one person messes up, the whole team accepts it. We will use mistakes to learn and grow. When one person has a great game, credit goes to the whole team. A team's strength is the ability of the team to work together, to take care of each other, to appreciate each other. Everybody good so far?"

We all nodded. We really just wanted to get our uniforms and schedules.

"I believe that on this team, you can learn everything really important in life — commitment, respect, teamwork and learning from mistakes."

Coach A paused. There was an awkward silence.

I am not sure I believe that, I thought. But . . . can I please have my jersey?

"Okay," Coach A continued, clapping her hands in front of her. "I will be meeting with each of you over the next two weeks to talk about your role on the team. As I mentioned at practice yesterday, practices will begin at four o'clock, Monday to Thursday. That will give you a half-hour break after school. Have a snack, catch up with your friends and show up ready to practice hard."

Coach A handed out a team jersey and a schedule to each player. The games started in two weeks. All the games except for one were at the same time as our practices, four o'clock. There was one six o'clock game. I didn't yet know how I would handle that, but I had the rest all figured out.

★★★

The weekend passed slowly, but finally Monday arrived.

"C'mon, Rory, walk faster," I commanded on the way home from school. I would get Rory home and put on some videos for him. I'd bribe him with the promise to play his favourite game each day when I got home. He would never know the difference. He always sat for two hours in front of that TV after school anyway. I told myself I didn't need to be there. He would be fine.

"Okay, Rory," I said. "I'll be right back. Just watch your shows and I'll come home and play with you."

He nodded absently, already so into his show that he barely knew I was there.

I opened the door and ran. I ran hard. It was

the only way I could make it back to school in time for practice. I got there in under ten minutes. I ran straight to the change room. I had left my shorts and T-shirt on under my school clothes to speed up the change. I whipped off my jeans and hoodie and ran out to the court. Coach A was just calling all the girls in. She looked over her shoulder at me as I ran to join the group.

"You should give yourself a few extra minutes, Miss Beck. You are cutting it pretty close."

"Yes, I'm sorry," I replied. "I will." I would have to find a way to be faster tomorrow.

Practice was okay. I was strong and I was fast. But the ball was a brick in my hands. I didn't think I would get a lot of playing time in games, but I was just happy to be part of the team, part of something. The excitement and energy of every girl was released and the gym felt electrified.

I had started out exhausted. By the end of the ninety-minute practice I felt like I was going to throw up. But I had no time to waste. I threw on my outdoor clothes and took off.

"Hey, Jo!" I heard Hala call after me. I ignored her and kept running.

I had fifteen minutes to get home and catch my breath. Then I had to act as if it was a day like any other when my mom got home from work. I had no time to go back and talk to Hala.

Tuesday, Wednesday, Thursday — I went through the same routine. I rushed my brother home, put on his favourite shows and bolted. I always bribed him with the promise to play Caterpillar. He was so obsessed with that game he would do anything for the chance to play. I told him this was our secret. I said if he ever told Mom, I would never be able to play Caterpillar with him again. He looked at me wide-eyed and asked, "Why?"

"Because I will be so upset that I will break that game into pieces." I didn't like threatening him, but I didn't feel I had a choice. I couldn't think about what would happen if Mom found out.

"I won't tell," he said. "I promise. Don't break my game."

"You keep our secret and your game is safe," I assured him.

"Okay."

By the next Monday, I had two minutes to spare before Coach A called everyone in to start practice. I was really getting into the routine and making the most of every minute.

At the end of practice, Coach A put up a schedule for a meeting with each player. My meeting was scheduled for the next Friday after school. I could not believe my luck. All the other girls were scheduled after a practice time. I would never be able to stay if Coach A had scheduled me in that time slot. Did she know?

No, she didn't know that I was leaving my little brother all alone for two hours every day. What would she do if she knew? I was not planning to let her find out.

★★★

Hey, Jo, Hala texted me that night. When r u meeting with Coach A?

Next Friday, u?

We met after practice today

Ya? What did she say?

She asked me about my role on the team. What I saw as my strengths. How I would contribute to the success of the team

What did u say?

I said I thought I was a good shooter

What did she say?

She agreed. She said that because I was on the team last year she saw me as a leader

Wow, really? That's great, I texted back.

Thanks. Gotta go get my homework done

Okay, TTYL

Oh BTW, why r u running off right after practice all the time? U r missing all the team stuff, the fun. U really should stick around a few minutes

I can't. My mom gets on my case. She wants me to help make dinner, set the table, play with my brother and stuff

Oh, that sucks. I'm sorry

Ya, not much I can do about it

I guess not. Bye

Bye

I felt sick. I had just lied to my best friend. I had thought about telling her the truth, but I couldn't risk it. She'd tell someone and my basketball days would be over. I told myself that some lies were just necessary. I took out my math homework and got started.

5 The Problem with RORY

"Okay, Rory," I said. "I have to go now." It was Tuesday after school. Rory and I had fallen into a good routine.

"But I want you to play Caterpillar with me."

"I will, Rory. I have to go now. But I will come back and play with you, just like I always do. I promise."

"But I want to play now."

"I can't play now. I will play with you when I get back."

"I don't want you to go."

"I have to. I'm sorry. I'm going to be late if I don't go. Your show is on, just watch it." I sat him down in front of the TV and flew out the door.

I ran faster than I had ever run before. I was going to be late. I knew it. Rory had been really slow coming home from school. I had given him a piggyback ride for the final two blocks because he refused to speed up.

Surprisingly, I arrived at school earlier than usual. The other girls were just finishing up in the change room and heading out onto the court. I looked up at the clock. I had run the mile back to school in eight minutes. All this running back and forth was making me more fit.

Coach A reminded us that our first game was coming up the next week, and then we were in a big tournament a few weeks after that. We spent a lot of time reviewing our offense. Coach A taught us how to read the other team's defense. We practised making hard cuts to get open for a pass. If our check was still right on us, we went the opposite way to get open. I learned this was called a "back door." She emphasized that we had to know what was going on close to the basket. She told us that if someone was open there, it was a gift basket and we had to see it.

Coach A was also very big on defense. We spent at least a half hour of every practice on it.

Coach A liked to play what she called an exciting game.

"Girls' basketball should be exciting to watch," she said. "Anyone who thinks otherwise should have their opinion changed after watching us play. Let's always look for the fast break, move the ball quickly. Let's wear out the other team until they can't keep up with us anymore. But," she paused, "never rush and make poor choices. It will cost you something every time. Sometimes it will cost just a basket or a foul, but other times, the whole game."

So much to know. My head was usually swimming by the end of practice.

As soon as practice was over, I grabbed my stuff and headed home. As I started running, I remembered how I had left my brother and sped up. I kept hearing Coach A's voice saying, *Never rush and make poor choices. It will cost you.* Had I rushed into my choices? The choice to lie? The choice to leave my brother? I wondered what my poor choices off the court were going to cost me.

I tried to tell myself that Rory had probably settled into his show. He'd probably forgotten all about whatever was bothering him earlier. But I couldn't shake the feeling that he had not. I sped up a little more, panic setting in.

"Rory, I'm home!" I shouted. I bent over to catch my breath.

"Rory!!" No answer.

I kicked off my shoes and ran into the living room. No Rory.

"Rory! Where are you?"

I heard a sound from his bedroom and ran to it, flinging open the door.

There was Rory, crying. He was sitting under the desk in his room with his favourite stuffed animal.

"Rory, what's wrong?" I went to him and reached out a hand. "Come out from under there. Come here."

Rory came out and flung himself into my arms. I held him and stroked his head for a long time until he stopped crying. I didn't know what had changed with him. I just knew it was now my problem.

I heard the back door open.

"Hey, guys. I'm home!" Mom called.

"Hi, Mom," I answered. I quickly found Rory's Caterpillar game, opened the game board and sat across from Rory on the floor. As soon as he saw we were playing, he smiled. I acted like we had been playing the game for hours.

Rory's back was to the door, so Mom couldn't see his red, puffy eyes when she peeked in the room. "Oh, there you are. Caterpillar again, eh?" she said.

Mom closed the door and headed to her room to change. She always worked long shifts. By the time she got home, she was usually pretty tired, but she insisted on making dinner. She said I was doing enough just taking care of Rory.

Guilt shot through me as I remembered that. I thought about how much she counted on me. But I forced myself to think of something else.

"Okay, Rory, your turn," I said.

Rory and I played for half an hour until Mom called us to dinner. Rory's eyes looked almost normal by then, but I made sure to be very chatty at dinner to distract Mom.

The next day Rory was slow coming home from school again. I gave him another piggyback ride for the last few blocks because I was running out of time. He hung on tight and leaned his little head in to protect himself from the wind.

"Okay, Rory," I gasped when I let him down inside the back door. "I have to go. I have no time to come in with you." I stopped to catch my breath. "Take off your stuff and turn on your show. We will play when I get back."

"No!! I wanna play now!" He started crying.

No, no, no. Not again. This had all been working so well.

"Please, Rory. Just go watch your show."

He sat in the back entrance, sobbing, all his stuff still on.

I opened the door and left him there. I started running. It felt so good to run. My breath came faster and faster, but my legs felt strong, powerful. I pushed forward until I saw the school. An image of Rory crying by the back door was stuck in my mind. I shook it away and told myself that he was safe, that it was okay. But I knew it wasn't. If Mom found out, she would never forgive me. And if Rory was upset enough, would he tell?

I stood in the gym, frozen. I couldn't risk it. I took a minute to catch my breath and then did what I knew I had to do.

I walked to the gym office where Coach A was getting her clipboard to begin practice.

"Coach," I began. "I think I should go home. I don't feel well." I held my stomach.

"Oh, I am sorry to hear that, Jo," Coach A said. "You do look very flushed. Do you need me to find someone to drive you home?"

"No, thanks, I can get home on my own. I'm really sorry. But it's these cramps, you know . . ."

"I do. Rest up and get healthy. We have a lot of games coming up."

"Thanks."

With that, I walked slowly to the gym door while the rest of the girls gathered around to start practice. As soon as I was out of sight, I ran. I was still tired from the last run, but I pushed myself to get home as fast as I could.

6 Problem **SOLVED**

I was glad I rushed home. When I got there, Rory was still sitting by the back door. All of his stuff was still on. His nose was running and snot was gathering in his scarf. He tried to catch his breath between sobs.

I held him. "I'm sorry, Rory. I am so sorry. I am here. Don't cry. I am here now."

I helped him get his snowsuit and boots off. I found his favourite stuffy and book and read to him. Still sobbing, he rested his head on my shoulder and listened to the story. What had changed? Why was Rory so upset when I left this time?

While I was reading the story, another story was playing out in my head. It was the story of me having to quit the team. I felt defeated.

Mom came home. We had dinner together and I spent the rest of the evening in my room.

Hey, what happened? I saw u talking to Coach today. r u ok? I looked at the text from Hala and put my phone back down. I heard several more messages come in, but I couldn't make myself answer them.

The next thing I knew, Rory was tugging at my arm. "Jo, get up."

I looked over at my clock. Eight-fifteen in the morning. I had forgotten to set my alarm.

I didn't care.

I looked at Rory. "No school today," I mumbled. "Go play."

"Yes, there is! Ms. Short said we were testing our cars today. I am going to miss it. I have to go. I want to test my car!"

I forced myself to get up.

"Okay, okay. Go get dressed, Rory."

I took my brother to school, but it was all I could do. I had no energy. I went back home and crawled into bed. I went back to school for 3:30 and picked up my brother. We walked home. I put on his show and lay down on the couch beside him.

★★★

It was Thursday. I was missing practice again and the next day I was supposed to meet with Coach A. No matter how I worked things in my mind, I didn't know how I was going to do it. I couldn't tell Mom what I had been doing. She would never trust me again. I couldn't tell anyone else. They would think I was a horrible person. I was a horrible person.

Problem Solved

I looked out the window and watched the snow falling gently. The kid next door, Ming, was coming home from school. He was in grade seven, just a year younger than me. Nice kid. We used to hang out with the other neighbourhood kids when I was younger, but I hardly ever saw him anymore. He went to the private school just a few blocks from our house.

I felt a small surge of hope, a new energy. I had an idea.

I found my password and logged into my bank account. I looked at the balance.

The summer before, I'd babysat for the family down the street every Saturday. They paid me well and even had me babysit evenings from time to time. I had saved the money, hoping to get myself a nicer phone.

Basketball meant more to me than a nice phone. So I started to plan out how I could use this money. If I paid Ming to watch Rory for two hours after school every day, I could keep playing for almost three months. I had already used some of the emergency money to pay my basketball fees, so I still had enough to take me through the season and playoffs. Maybe I could convince Ming to do it for a little less so that I would have enough for the whole season. I played with the different amounts I could pay him and how long it would allow me to play.

"Hey, Rory," I began. "Do you remember Ming?"

Rory looked up right away and nodded.

"Let's go for a visit."

"Okay," Rory replied eagerly. It had been a couple of years since he had been in Ming's house, but he must have remembered the mountain of Lego Ming had.

We headed over to Ming's house and rang the bell. Ming peeked out to see who it was before answering. He was usually home for a couple of hours by himself after school until his own parents came home from work. Maybe he would like some company.

"Hey, Jo." He looked at me as if to say, *What do you want?*

"Uh, how are you?" I asked.

"Good, you?"

"I'm good. We're good." This was feeling awkward. "I was wondering, Ming, if maybe you would like to make a little extra money?"

I saw I had his interest. Ming's parents did not give him an allowance and he was too young for a real job.

"I'm listening," he said.

I told him about needing someone to watch Rory and offered my lowest amount to him.

"Sure," he said right away.

I wondered if he might have done it for even less money.

After working out the details, I told him it would start the next day. Ming insisted that he would only watch Rory if it was at his own house. I could not afford to lose this deal, so I agreed. Ming got home from school around four o'clock every day. This was the only problem. He would have to come and get Rory from our house at four o'clock, and I had to leave to get to basketball before that. This meant Rory would be alone for about ten minutes. Another thing it meant was that our back door would stay unlocked until I got home from practice. I could live with that. Rory was so excited to play with Ming every day that he agreed.

We went home and I started to think about my meeting with Coach A the next day. Maybe this was going to work out after all.

7 MISSING OUT

Where have u been? Hala texted. I had not gotten back to her. Why aren't u answering my texts? Is everything ok?

Then, I don't know whether to be mad at u or worried

I'm ok, Hala. Sorry, I was feeling really crappy earlier

OMG, you could have just said so. I saw u talk to coach on Wednesday, then you weren't at school today. None of us knew what was going on. We thought something horrible had happened. You have been sick a lot. Have you gone to the doctor?

I'm sorry, Hala. I didn't mean to worry anyone

Well, r u ok? I mean, what's wrong?

I'm okay now, just bad stomach cramps. I will be at school tomorrow. I have my meeting with Coach A after school

O right. B ready to tell her what you think u can do for the team!

Right. I better start thinking about that

Defense! You're great on defense

I'm not that good

U R!!!

Thanks Hala. I have nothing else, so I guess that is what I'll say

Ok. c u tomorrow. Glad u r ok.

★★★

When I got to school the next day, Hala was waiting for me. She gave me a big hug.

"I'm so glad you are back," she said.

"Ya, me too," I answered. I wanted to tell her all about Ming and Rory, about how I had solved my problem, but I couldn't. If I wanted to keep playing, no one could know what I was doing. So, I didn't tell Hala anything. Before long, we were back to our routine, chatting and laughing. At lunch we sat with the other girls from the basketball team. I had always been a one- or two-friend kind of person. It was hard to hang out and chat when I always had to go pick up my brother and go straight home after school. Now, sitting with my teammates, the topic at lunch was how hot Rachel's older brother was. He had been in our school a few years ago but was now in high school. Rachel couldn't believe we were all talking about him.

"Ew, stop it!" she cried. "He's my brother! Don't, just don't." She made a funny face and we all laughed.

It felt good to be back. I felt better than I had in a

long time. I would no longer have to feel guilty about leaving my brother alone. I would not have to lie about being sick so that I could stay home with him. I felt hopeful.

I smiled and took a bite of my sandwich.

No one had to know. It was all going to be okay.

When the end of the day finally arrived, I quickly picked up Rory and nervously headed to the gym. I gave Rory a sucker and told him to wait for me on the bench outside the gym.

"I'll be back in a few minutes. Wait here."

Rory nodded. He had already unwrapped the sucker and stuck it in his mouth.

I slowly walked over to the phys ed office, where Coach A was waiting.

"Jo, it's good to see you. Are you feeling better?" Coach A invited me to have a seat.

"Yes, thank you. I am so sorry about all the practices I missed."

"What's important is that you are feeling better. We have our first game soon."

I nodded.

"Jo," she continued. "How do you see yourself contributing to the team? What do you think your strengths are?"

I knew this was coming, but it still felt weird to talk about what I was good at. "Um, I think I play good defense."

Coach A smiled. "I think you're right. You are fast and you anticipate well. Anything else?"

I shrugged.

"Jo, this is your first year playing basketball, right?"

I nodded again.

"Some of the other girls play on community club teams, especially before they are old enough to play on the school team. This gives them some skills before they ever even attend a tryout." She paused. "I think you have great potential, Jo. You work really hard. Even at the end of practice, you are still going strong."

I waited for more. If only she knew why.

"You do lack the fundamentals, though."

Now this was sounding more like me.

"I know," I said. "I know I am not very good, but I really love to play."

"I never said you weren't good, Jo. There are some very strong parts to your game — defense, as you mentioned." Coach A paused again. "Jenna also needs work on her shooting and ball handling. She has agreed to come every Friday after school to work on these skills. I was hoping you could join us."

I started calculating the extra money I would have to pay Ming. I wasn't sure I had enough, but I couldn't pass up this chance. "Yes, I can do that."

"Okay, we will start next Friday, four to five-thirty."

"Thank you, Coach A."

I felt light and free as I headed toward home.

My meeting had been less than ten minutes. Rory and I took our time for a change and I found myself enjoying the walk. I could feel my phone vibrating in my pocket, but I waited until I got home to check it. I smiled. Things were looking up.

When we got home I pulled out my phone.

So how did your meeting go? Hala had texted.

Good. I said what u told me to say about defense, I replied.

Jenna and I are going to see a movie, want to come? Tonight?

Ya, my mom is driving. Can we pick u up at 7:30?

I don't think I can go. I thought about how I would need every cent I had to pay Ming. Maybe next time.

C'mon. We haven't been out for ages. What's up?

I have to take care of my brother, I lied. I couldn't tell her I had no money because she knew that wasn't true.

What? Why?

My mom has some retirement party.

Lying was getting easier and easier. I barely had to think about it anymore. The lies just came to me. I felt a tinge of jealousy that Hala and Jenna would be going out and having fun without me. But I couldn't risk telling Hala the real reason I couldn't go.

Okay, TTYL

Yep, bye. Have fun, I texted, but I realized I didn't really want her to have a good time. I wanted her to miss me and wish I was there. I pushed my thoughts aside and left my phone by my bed. I could hear Mom coming in the door.

Before too long we were sitting down to eat dinner. Mom looked tired, as she always did on Friday nights after working all week.

"I'll clean up, Mom," I offered when dinner was over. "You go relax."

She didn't say anything, just gave me a hug. She went into the living room and turned on the TV. As soon as I was finished the dishes, I started thinking about how much fun Hala and Jenna were probably having. I thought about how easy it would be for Hala to replace me as her best friend. I started thinking about what a rotten friend I had been lately. Not answering her texts, lying to her, not going out with her. The more I thought about it, the more I saw no reason why Hala would even want me as a friend.

Around ten, I decided to send a text and see how they were doing.

Hey, I wrote. How was the movie?

Hala responded in seconds. Awesome! It was so funny. You've got to go see it.

So, r u home now? I really wanted her to say yes. A part of me needed to know that she and Jenna were not still having fun without me.

Yep, just got home when u texted

I sighed in relief. Maybe I was over-thinking things.

Jenna and I are just going to make sundaes before her dad picks her up!

My heart sank. Oh, yum. Wish I was there, I responded. And I did. I really wished I was there. I told myself that I could do all kinds of things when basketball season was over. Summer would be here before we knew it and we could hang out all the time. But I had the nagging fear of losing Hala's friendship.

We ended our conversation. I went to the living room to watch TV with mom. Her favourite show was on, but she was sound asleep. I covered her with a blanket and went to my room.

8 MISTAKES

"Okay, girls," began Coach A. "Our first game is starting in ten minutes. I want you to relax and focus on the things we have been practising. Always square up to the basket, read the defense and get the ball up the court quickly. Don't be afraid to make mistakes. You are all going to make them. Use them to improve your play."

Everyone was excited. We stood there, huddled around the coach and her clipboard, proudly wearing our uniforms. Hala was like an animal waiting to get out of a cage, taking small side-to-side steps with her feet. She listened closely to every word the coach was saying, nodding her head.

"I will play all of you today," Coach A continued. "In the first half, you will play in equal shifts. In the second half, I will play those of you who show me you are ready for the challenge and the pressure of the second half. Okay, we will start with Kisha, Rachel, Hala, Della and Jae."

She assigned positions. Before we knew it, the buzzer sounded for the warm-up time to end and the game to begin.

"One minute, Coach," the ref said as she walked over to the bench.

I was relieved that I did not have to go on first. I felt better watching for the first few minutes to get an idea of what to do. Rachel played the same position that I usually did, so I would watch her closely.

I saw the ref point to the direction each team was shooting before she tossed up the jump ball. Kisha easily tapped it back to Rachel, who started dribbling up the court. Hala was already cutting to the basket, but Rachel didn't see her.

"Heads up. See the basket," Coach shouted from the side.

Hala cut back out for the ball and Rachel got it to her. Hala drove hard to the basket and left her check in the dust. I watched Rachel's movements for several minutes as the team went up and down the court. After four minutes, the score was 10–6 for us.

"Okay, girls, sub in." Coach A had already told us who would be on the next line, so we were ready to go. We waited for the refs to wave us in, then ran onto the court.

Grace threw the ball in to me. I automatically turned to the basket and looked to see if someone was open.

Nothing.

I started to dribble and saw Grace cut out. I passed the ball. The defense jumped in, got the ball and headed toward our basket.

It all happened so fast. I didn't have time to think. I did the same thing the next time I got the ball.

I didn't get the ball again that shift. Coach called me over when our shift was done.

"Jo," she began, "great effort out there. You made some mistakes, as I said we all would. What did you learn?"

I just sat there. What had I learned? I wasn't sure.

"Why didn't Grace get the ball you passed to her?" she asked.

"Her check stole it," I answered quickly.

"Why?" she asked.

"Uh, it was a bad pass?" I wasn't sure what she wanted me to say.

"Yes, why?" She wasn't at all angry. "When someone is overplayed, what do you look for? We practised this last week."

The light bulb in my head went on. "The back door pass!"

"Atta girl. Look for it next time," she encouraged.

I nodded and moved back with my line down the bench. In a couple of minutes we would be on again.

No one was passing me the ball. I can't say I blamed them. I had thrown it away too many times.

I watched my check closely. Her teammate passed her the ball and she put it down right away. I paid attention to the rhythm of the dribble. Just after it bounced on the floor the third time, I tapped the ball with my hand. The ball was loose! I ran hard to get it and looked down the court. I saw Kristen's hand in the air as she ran toward the basket. I threw the ball to her and watched her score an easy lay-up.

"Nice steal. Way to look up the court," Coach A called.

That seemed to renew the team's faith in me. After a few minutes, I got a pass. I in-turned and saw Grace cutting in. This time I saw that her check was overplaying her. I faked the pass and Grace went the opposite direction for a perfect back door. I got her the ball. Gift basket.

"Good read!" I heard Coach A shout from the bench.

We ended up winning the game 40–34. Hala had 21 points and the rest were spread out among a few other girls. We all cheered and hugged each other.

I looked at the clock. The game hadn't taken as long as our practices. It was only five-fifteen and the game was over. I could hang out with the team and take my time today.

"Hala, you were awesome!" I said as we left the gym.

"So were you," she said. "You would never know that was your first game."

"I don't know about that," I answered. "But I did have fun."

Mistakes

"Yaaa!!!" she laughed, and I laughed too. We flung our arms around each other's shoulders and walked into the change room.

I realized I was thinking about basketball all the time. I couldn't wait for practice. When I wasn't at practice I was practising in my head, going over what I had learned. I was seeing myself stealing the ball and scoring lay-ups and dreaming about Hala and me playing on the high school team together. I loved how Coach A encouraged us to not be afraid to make mistakes, but to use mistakes as a way to grow and learn. Was I making a mistake choosing the team over Rory and my mom? And if it was a mistake, was it a good mistake as long as I learned something in the end?

9 Muscle MEMORY

"You seem to be in a good mood today," Mom said as I helped set the table for dinner.

"Ya, I guess," I answered.

"Something good happen at school today?" she asked.

"Not really." I couldn't think of anything I could tell her about that would explain why I was so happy.

Of course, I knew it was basketball. The fun of the game lingered. I was looking forward to Friday when Coach A was going to work with me and Jenna.

"Well, it's nice." Mom smiled. "I know I expect a lot of you. And I don't tell you enough how much I appreciate it." She paused. "Sometimes I feel that you are unhappy."

"I'm good, Mom." It was true. I didn't have to lie about that. I finally felt that everything was working out. As long as Rory could keep our little secret, no one else had to know and my life was fine. Rory loved going to Ming's house. Ming was like a more grown-up version of my little brother. I think he loved all the same toys and games that Rory did. Rory was good company for him. I told them both that, for reasons I could not tell them, it was best that no one else knew about our arrangement. I told them that if anyone else found out, it would be over. I knew neither of them wanted that. It was a great deal for everyone. So far, they had managed to keep their mouths shut about it.

Mom, Rory and I sat down for dinner. Mom and I were sick of pasta, so Mom had made tacos for us. Delicious, and a welcome change.

"Thanks for dinner, Mom," I said when we were done. "That was so good. Nice to have a break from pasta."

We both smiled.

"You can say that again!" she laughed. "I think we all have pasta coming out of our ears!"

★★★

The next couple of days went by quickly. Before I knew it, it was Friday. At the end of the school day I picked up Rory as usual. I got him home and ran back to school for my practice with Coach A.

"Okay, girls. I want you to know why I am giving up my Friday to work with you." Coach A picked up a basketball and held it in her hand. "You both work super hard but do not have as much basketball experience as some of the other girls. This affects your ability to act without thinking. What I am hoping we can do here is create some muscle memory. We will do things over and over and over again, until you can do them without thinking. That way you can focus more on the game strategies and teamwork."

Jenna and I looked at each other and then back to Coach A.

"We are going to start with shooting. I don't want you to have to stop in the middle of a game to think about your feet, where your elbow is, how you are holding the ball, your follow-through. We will work on these things now, so that your body starts to remember automatically. Okay, go grab a ball and let's get started."

Jenna and I both ran to get a ball.

"Now, triple threat position. Show me."

Jenna and I both remembered this position from team practice. We stood with our knees bent, feet shoulder-width apart and the ball held close.

"Good. From here you can pass, shoot or dribble. Today we are going to work on shooting. When you receive the ball I want you to catch it in this position. Now let's go over the basics of a good shot."

From there Coach A broke down the sequence of body movements needed to go from triple threat position to taking a shot. She had us work on different drills, starting from triple threat position.

"Okay, we have half an hour left. Now when do

you think you would take a shot without starting from triple threat position?"

I had no idea. We both shrugged.

"Well, when would you not consider dribbling or passing, just shooting?"

Silence.

She waited.

Okay, she wasn't going to just tell us.

"Right under the basket," I finally said, realizing the obvious.

"Yes, exactly. When you get a rebound right under the basket, or you receive a pass there, you are always looking to shoot. You will keep the ball high and complete your shot from there. Use the backboard. It's there to help you. The bank shot is your path to success down low."

We spent the last bit of time giving each other high passes right under the basket. Coach A showed us how to put our target hand high to receive the pass. From there, we just squared up to the basket and banked it in. I got a funny image of Ming as my backboard, my help to get me where I wanted to go. My whole path to playing basketball felt like a bank shot. I saw how well it worked. Jenna and I sunk shot after shot.

Soon we were done. We both felt great about what we had learned.

"How are you getting to the tournament next weekend?" Jenna asked while we were changing to go home. "My mom and dad are planning to watch all of the games. Hala is coming with us. We have room for you, too, if you want."

The tournament. I couldn't believe I had not stopped to think about how I was going to explain that to Mom. I quickly accepted the ride. I could not risk missing the tournament because I had no way to get there. It was at the other end of town.

"Sure. That would be great," I said, trying to seem casual.

"I think we get the schedule next week. I will let you know what time we will pick you up."

"Thanks, Jenna. That's great."

We chatted a little more about the tournament. It would be one game on Friday night, then two or three games on Saturday.

"See you, Jenna." I waved good-bye as we headed home in opposite directions.

I started my run home. I was mad at myself for not figuring this all out earlier. I had to come up with a plan — fast. What if the Friday game was not at four o'clock? How would I explain to Mom that I would be gone Friday evening and all day Saturday? My first impulse was to come up with a lie. Muscle memory? Were the lies becoming automatic, just like Coach A hoped my shot would become? At first I had to really think about the lies, but now they seemed to roll off my tongue. Maybe muscle memory wasn't always a good thing.

I finally decided that the best thing would be to tell Mom the truth about the tournament. She knew that Hala and I were best friends. I would tell her that I wanted to go to watch Hala play. Since it was so far away, I would just stay the whole day. Mostly true. Mom would be home from work Friday evening and Saturday, so Rory would be fine. I relaxed a little. I would mention it at dinner.

10 A Dash of TRUTH

"Mom, I have something to ask," I began as we sat down for dinner. "The girls' basketball team is in a tournament next weekend. Jenna's dad is driving and said I could go with them to watch. I really want to watch Hala play. Is that okay?"

"I guess so," Mom replied. "I didn't know you were interested in basketball. You have never mentioned it before."

"Mom, don't you remember I wanted to try out last year?" I could not believe she had forgotten. "I even tried asking you again this year."

"Oh, yeah, right. I do remember something about that. What time is the game?"

"Well, there will be a few games and I don't think they have the schedule yet. Can I let you know?"

"When you get the schedule, we will see if it works. Maybe you can just go for one game."

"Mom, I can't ask Jenna's dad to drive me home in between games. I would stay all day."

"You might get bored, Jo. That could be a very long day."

"That's okay. I don't mind."

Mom shrugged. She repeated that we would talk about it again when I had more information.

Okay, it sounded like she would let me go. But I could not know for sure until that schedule came out. I kept my fingers crossed. I would do whatever I had to. I was not missing that tournament.

It was a pretty uneventful weekend. I cleaned up my room, did a little homework, watched some movies and texted Hala. I told her about my shooting practice. She told me that Coach A did that every year. She would work with a few girls who had a good attitude but lacked some of the basics, to try and boost their skills.

Busy week, texted Hala. Game Wednesday, then tournament on the weekend.

I would play every day if I could

Jenna said u r coming with us to the tournament?

Yep

Must be nice to have parents who want to watch you play?

I know

My mom and dad ask about the games when I get home. But they have no interest in going. I swear, Mo and Maram take up all of their extra time these days. Your mom isn't interested either?

Hala often told me about the problems her older brother was having in school. I knew how her older sister counted on her mom and dad to help with her daughter. They didn't seem to have a lot of time or energy for Hala. I knew at times it bothered her. I was not the only one with a tired mother.

No, I answered. My mom is just tired a lot. She works, comes home and makes dinner, relaxes for a couple of hours, then goes to bed

It felt good to be having a conversation that wasn't full of lies. Of course the truth was that my mom didn't even know I was playing.

Ya, Jenna's really lucky. Her parents go to all her stuff. She just takes it for granted tho, u know

Well at least we will have some fans at the game

Ya, Rachel's brother will be there too. He just got his licence and now their parents make him pick her up for all of her practices and games. I guess they are too busy too

Okay, three fans so far

LOL, a few more than that I hope

Can't wait . . . SO EXCITED!

Me 2, TTYL

The tournament schedule was handed out after practice on Tuesday. Our Friday game was at six o'clock. That meant we had to leave for the game at five o'clock. The wheels in my head were turning as I ran home from practice to pick up Rory. If I went to the game, it meant that I wouldn't be back in time to get Rory from Ming's. I decided to try a little truth again.

"Mom, I got the schedule today."

"Oh, good. So what time will Jenna's parents pick you up on Saturday?"

"Well," I began, "there's actually a game on Friday too. I want to go."

"Jo, you know you have to look after your brother. If you are going to be there all day on Saturday, I think that will be enough."

"Please, Mom. I know I am supposed to watch Rory. But I was talking to Ming today and he said Rory could come over there. Ming could watch Rory till you got home."

"Jo, I am not paying Ming to watch Rory when you are perfectly able to do it. Besides, you know how Rory can be. If he doesn't want to go, you'll have a fight on your hands. You will spend all of Saturday at the tournament. What is the big deal about going on Friday?"

"I just don't get out much on the weekends. The tournaments are really fun and exciting. There will be lots of other fans too. And you don't have to worry about the money. I will pay Ming. I have money saved up from last summer, remember? And I promise, if Rory makes a fuss and doesn't want to go, I'll stay home." Little did Mom know that I was sure Rory would not put up a fuss.

Mom stood there for a while. Then she rolled her eyes and said, "Okay, if it's that important to you and you are paying Ming, go ahead. Just don't make a habit of this, okay?"

Too late for that. Sorry, Mom.

"Thanks, Mom," I said. Another weight off, another problem solved.

Our second game of the season was coming up and I wanted my mind to be clear to think about basketball.

★★★

The team we played for our second game was really quite bad. We were able to fast break on them over and over again. They just couldn't keep up. They also only had seven players, and we had twelve. Coach A constantly changed the lines so we were going hard the entire first half.

At halftime the score was 40–3.

"Okay, girls," Coach A began. "We need to set some new goals this half. I don't want you fast breaking anymore. You have shown you can do it and the other team is completely exhausted. Two of their best players are injured and another one quit just before the game. I consider it a part of sportsmanship to never run a team into the ground. They are having enough trouble keeping their team together. It is now our job to keep them from getting too discouraged."

What was she saying? We were also responsible for how the other team felt?

"You are all going to get a lot of playing time on the weekend. I am going to play the new players more now, as they may get less time on the weekend. You will work on your passing. This will be your challenge. You are not allowed to shoot the ball until every player has received and given a pass. That means that we will be making at least five passes before shooting each and every time down the court." She paused. "On defense, no steals. Work hard at moving your feet and getting into the right position. But do not steal the ball. You will allow them to make all of their passes. You will allow them to dribble, while keeping good defensive position. If they shoot, hands straight up, no blocks."

The buzzer sounded to end the halftime break.

"Okay, let's go!" Coach A clapped her hands and told us who was going on the court.

I got a lot of playing time that half, and a lot of practice with passing. Most of the time we were able to make the passes, but they did steal the ball a couple of times. The final score was 65–30.

"Great job, girls!" Coach A said after the game. "You showed a great deal of discipline out there. The footwork was good and you really worked hard at getting into good defensive position. You allowed the other team to feel good about themselves and hopefully they want to keep playing. I know it's a lot more fun to score points. But we always have to keep others in mind when we set our goals. Today, we changed our goal to benefit both us and our opponents. You showed discipline and respect."

Ahh, yes, respect. She had talked about it in our first team meeting.

"All right. One more practice tomorrow before the tournament," Coach A's voice interrupted my thoughts. "Go home, relax, eat well and get a good sleep tonight. I need you all healthy and rested up."

I did exactly what Coach A told us to, after running home to get my brother. It was a quiet, relaxing evening at home. All I could think about was the tournament. Friday just could not come fast enough.

11 THE TOURNAMENT

On Friday I got my brother to Ming's. I made sure Ming understood that, when my mom came to get Rory at six o'clock, he had to act as if this was the first time he had ever watched Rory. He couldn't be making comments about when Rory was over last or anything like that. I reminded Ming that the money train would be stopping if Mom found out.

I reminded Rory that if he told Mom, he would not be playing with Ming anymore after school. Rory had grown even more fond of Ming and I knew he wouldn't tell on purpose. I just hoped it wouldn't accidentally slip out.

I headed home quickly. I got my backpack and waited for Jenna's parents to pick me up. They had decided to leave a little sooner to catch an earlier game. The team playing before us was our first game on Saturday, and we all wanted to see what they were like.

When I saw the car pull up in front of my house, I ran outside. I felt a sense of relief that everything had worked out. And I felt a sense of excitement for the game.

We arrived at the gym during halftime of the game before ours. Coach A usually met with the team about ten minutes before our warm-up started, so we settled into the bleachers and watched the third quarter of the game. The teams were both very good. The team that was winning had a couple of girls that looked six feet tall and a very speedy guard who shot and passed well. That team was fast breaking for most of their points. There were three girls who were doing everything. It was hard to say if the rest of them had any skills or not. The opposing team didn't appear to have any superstars, but they could all play, even the girls who came in off the bench.

Rachel walked in with her brother. He found a spot by himself in a corner of the bleachers and took out his phone while Rachel joined us. She rolled her eyes as she watched several of the girls look over at him and smile.

When the fourth quarter started, Coach A called us together.

"Okay, girls. You can see that there are some very strong teams in this tournament. Don't let that scare you. I want you to keep playing hard. Believe in yourselves and your teammates, and don't be afraid to take chances. We are using this tournament to get experience and to learn from our mistakes. I don't know much about the team we are playing tonight, so I will give you some tips during the game once I see what they do."

She told us who was on the first two lines. We got back inside the gym with one minute left on the clock in the game before our own. It was a close game. The Hornets, the team with the tall girls, ended up winning by eleven points.

The two teams shook hands and grabbed their stuff from the bench as we began our warm-up. Before we knew it, our game was starting.

I got to go on first. I got the jump ball tip from Kisha. I looked up the court to see Hala racing to the basket. I threw her the ball and she went in for an easy two points.

Hala nodded a thank-you to me for the pass. That small gesture made my heart swell. We found our checks as the other team passed in the ball. We were not allowed to press until the final quarter, so their guard easily brought the ball up and over centre.

"Tough D, now, girls!" Coach A shouted from the bench.

The girl I was checking was dribbling the ball. I watched her closely and listened for the rhythm of the ball's bounce on the hardwood floor. "Thump, thump, thump . . . and I was in there. A quick sideways tap on the ball made it come loose. In two quick steps I was dribbling it down the court toward the basket.

There was no one there. This was my first fast break. I ran as hard as I could, but I had trouble controlling the ball. Before I knew it, the player I stole the ball from was back on defense. My chance for an easy lay-up was gone.

Out of the corner of my eye I saw Jenna sprinting down the other side of the key. Her hand was up for the pass, just like we had been working on the Friday before. I picked up the ball and aimed just ahead of her target hand. She wasn't quite as fast as I thought and she had to scramble hard to keep it from going out of bounds. By then most of the other girls were back and we set up our offense.

"Good try. Way to keep your head up, Jo!" Coach A called from the bench. "Look for your cutters now."

Before I knew it, my shift was over and I was on the bench cheering on the next line. The team we were playing was pretty good, but nothing like the two teams that had played before us. We had a fairly easy win and everyone got lots of time on the court. We were all smiles and laughs in the change room following the game.

As I sat in the car for the ride home I started thinking about how I looked. My face was red. I was sweaty. I looked like I had just played a basketball game. I needed to get into the house without Mom having a good look at me. I had to wash up, maybe hang out for a bit in my room before I spent any time with her.

As luck would have it, Mom was reading Rory a bedtime story when I walked in. I just shouted a greeting and headed to my room. I washed up, changed into my pajamas and looked at myself in the mirror. Wow, I thought. I am still a little red. I checked the clock. Our game had ended more than an hour ago. I looked in the mirror again. I splashed more cold water on my face and decided not to join Mom and Rory. I could hear them in his room now.

I lay down on my bed and opened the book I was reading.

Mom popped her head in after finishing up with Rory. "How was the game?" she asked.

I kept the book in front of my face and peeked over the top to look at her. "It was great. We — they won. Hala played really well. Tomorrow they have to play a really good team, though, so it's going to be a lot tougher."

"Well, that's good. I mean that they won tonight. What time will you be leaving tomorrow?"

"I'm getting picked up at eight o'clock in the morning."

"Wow, that's early for you on a Saturday. It must be exciting." She laughed. "I don't know when you are planning to be back tomorrow. But if Rory and I are out, it's because I have taken him skating. Make sure you take a key just in case."

"Okay, thanks."

And with that, Mom closed my door and left me with my book. I read the same page at least three times before I gave up. I replayed moments of the game over and over in my head. I imagined playing the Hornets the next day and wondered who Coach A would get to check those tall girls. Hala and Kisha were both about five-foot-nine, but we didn't have any really tall girls. At five-foot-four I wasn't super short, but I was certainly not able to check one of the big girls. I had a feeling I would be checking that speedy guard and my stomach began to flutter. She was fast and smart. It was going to be a tough game.

It took a while for me to fall asleep. But when I did, my sleep was deep. I continued to play basketball in my dreams. When I woke up, I felt like I had just been through the warm-up. I was ready to play.

12 Watch and LEARN

Saturday morning, Jenna's mom and dad were right on time. I hugged Mom and ran out to the car.

"I am so nervous," Jenna said.

"Ya, did you see how tall those two girls are?" Hala added.

"I know. And that other girl! I counted four baskets just in that one quarter we watched!" I said.

"Coach is going to make you check her," Hala said.

"Yeah, I was afraid of that," I answered.

"You can do it," Hala encouraged. She was always so positive. Sometimes I wondered why she had such faith in me.

★★★

Hala was right about the checks.

"Jo and Rachel," Coach began in our pregame meeting. "You will be checking number Four. She is one of the top players in the province right now. It will be a challenge. I need to tell you that you will not be able to stop her from taking shots or making passes. What you can do is take away the easy shots and passes. She is a great ball handler, but she is right-handed and she prefers to go right. Take away her drive to the right side. Make her shoot off a left-handed dribble. As soon as she picks up the ball get tight on her. No easy passes."

Sure. No problem.

"Hala, Kisha, Della, you will be checking the tall girls, numbers Twenty-one and Fourteen. You need to do your best to deny them the ball. If they get the ball in the key, they will keep it high and just shoot over you. So play in front of them when they cut into the key. It is very important that all of you get on your checks tight when the ball is dead. We cannot allow easy passes or they will just lob it in over your head."

We all just stared at her.

"Okay, girls. Let's get out there!"

We warmed up and the game started.

I was on first, with Kisha, Hala, Jae and Kristen. The Hornets won the jump ball and we found our checks. Number Four had the ball. As I got into position to play defense, she looked like she was going to stop and pick up the ball. I moved toward her to stop the pass and she blew by me, going in for an easy lay-up.

"Wait till she picks up the ball, Jo," Coach A reminded me from the bench.

The next time down the court, number Four was dribbling hard to the right. I overplayed her, taking away the right side. She crossed the ball over to the left so fast I didn't have time to adjust my position. She just drove past me. Kristen came to help and her check went straight to the basket, receiving an easy pass from number Four to score another two points.

At the end of the quarter I came off. The score was 10–2.

"Good job, Jo," Coach A said. "You're doing great. She's tough to check."

I nodded and watched the next line. I wanted to be able to play like number Four. I couldn't take my eyes off her. So many times she looked like she was going to stop. Then, just as Rachel came closer, she would drive by, leaving Rachel in the dust.

Smart, I thought. Then I had an idea. Next shift I would see if it worked.

Coach A put Hala and me on again with about two minutes left in the half. Kisha was called for three seconds in the key. The Hornets inbounded the ball to number Four, who started dribbling up the court. I was not going to be beat again. She dribbled up fast, then stopped short, as though she was going to pick up the ball. I jabbed my right foot toward her like I was going to try to get the ball. Then I backed up fast, ready for her to try to beat me. When she saw me jab toward her, she put her shoulder down and dribbled hard, but

I was ready. I tapped the ball with my left hand, then raced after it and dribbled forward with my right hand. I was all alone, but I could feel her right behind me. I went in for a lay-up and watched as the ball bounced from one side of the rim to the other before dropping through the net. The bench went wild.

"Way to go, Jo!" several girls shouted.

"Nice steal!"

"WOOOOHOO!!!" was followed by whistling.

I felt joy bubbling up inside me. What a feeling!

I turned around and ran back to play defense as the Hornets had already inbounded the ball and were heading up the court.

The halftime buzzer sounded and the score was 16–4.

I wondered if the Hornets' coach would be like Coach A, getting the girls to stop fast breaking and let us make a pass or two. When the second half started, I found out that he was not that kind of coach. The Hornets seemed more determined than ever. When the fourth quarter started, they were ahead 34–16. They began to press. Coach A was not impressed. I could see her shaking her head and mumbling something as she glared at the other coach.

I could tell Hala had paid attention to her check's strengths and weaknesses. Number Fourteen always liked to take one dribble before shooting. So Hala hopped into that lane as soon as her check in-turned.

She got a couple of steals that way, and number Fourteen was starting to get frustrated.

The coach started yelling at her. "Don't put the ball down, Kayla. Just in-turn and shoot!"

Kayla tried that the next time down the court, but she was used to her routine and did not get away a good shot. Kristen got the rebound and passed it out to Grace, who was already sprinting down the court. The pass was a little short, and Grace had to reach back to get it. But she still had enough time to take a few dribbles and go in for an easy basket. The score was 34–18.

The crowd went wild again.

Coach A kept giving us tips, and we got a little better as the game went on. Still, we lost 40–30.

"I am so impressed by you all," Coach A started her post-game speech. "That was a really tough game and you girls never gave up. You watched and learned. You even outscored them in the last quarter, fourteen to six. You learned from your mistakes. I am so proud!" She put her hand to her heart as she said this.

We were bruised and battered, but we felt pretty good. Coach A had that gift. She could make us all feel good, even when we lost.

Our next game was at two o'clock. We had brought lunches and snacks, so we sat in the bleachers to chat and eat while the next games were being played. We didn't see any other team that looked as good as the one we had just played.

Bank Shot

We played at two o'clock and won quite easily. Then we played again in the third place final at four-thirty. This game was close. It ended with us up by six points. The two teams without any losses in their pool met in the final. Coach A suggested we stay and watch if we could.

Rachel didn't stay. I was sure her brother did not want to hang around any longer than he had to.

"Bye." Rachel looked kind of sad as she turned around and waved. "See you Monday."

I felt bad for her. I understood what it felt like to miss the fun of hanging out with the team.

The game was starting. Coach A encouraged us to cheer for good plays, not for either team.

"Don't cheer for the other team just because the Hornets beat you. Watch, learn and appreciate good basketball."

Ooo, that would be hard. We all wanted to cheer against the Hornets. But we did what Coach A asked, and we could hear her doing the same. It felt good. I found myself watching for the love of basketball, not with the desire for revenge. The Hornets won quite easily. No surprise there. I couldn't even imagine there being a better grade eight girls' team in the city. If there was a better team, we were not ready to play them, not yet.

13 THE SCARE

At Monday's practice, Coach A had some specific things she wanted to work on with us. We practised hard, still running on the excitement from the tournament.

I was about to run home to get Rory. This routine had been working out really well. I barely even thought about it anymore. It's just what I did — muscle memory.

Coach A called me over.

"Yes, Coach." I walked back toward her.

"Jo, I won't keep you long. I just thought you might be interested in attending a summer basketball camp. It can really help get your skills and confidence up."

"Summer camp?" I'd had no idea that such a thing existed.

"Yes. As soon as the information comes out, I'll make sure you get it."

"Thanks. That sounds great. I'd love to play in the summer."

Coach nodded to the door where Matt was waiting for Rachel. "Matt went after his grade eight year. It really helped prepare him. He is a starter this year on his high school varsity team."

I looked over at Matt. He looked up and Coach A waved at him. He waved back with a big smile.

"I am sure he'd tell you about it if you asked him. He loves talking basketball. I think he loves the sport about as much as you do." Coach A laughed.

"Thanks, Coach." I headed for the exit.

"Great game on Saturday." Matt smiled as I walked past him.

I looked up and then behind me. No one there. He was talking to me.

"Oh," I fumbled. "Thanks." I scurried out.

Matt, a varsity player, had complimented my play.

I ran to Ming's with a light heart. I pretended I was the best basketball player in the city. That all the girls my age were talking about me, like I was their idol.

Rory and I sauntered home. Rory chatted away about the huge Lego city he and Ming had been building.

"I want to tell Mom," he began.

"No! Rory, you can't. I told you. If Mom finds out you are going over to Ming's, you won't be able to go any more."

"Why? Is Ming bad? Doesn't Mom like him?"

"No, it's not that." I really didn't want to tell Rory about basketball. It was scary enough thinking that at any minute he might tell Mom about going to Ming's every day. So far, he had kept the secret. Rory really liked going over to Ming's. I think maybe he felt "seen" when he was with Ming, the way basketball made me feel. Rory would do anything to keep that feeling.

Mom came home soon after we got there.

"Jo, could you please get dinner started?" Mom asked. "I want to shovel the walk before dinner."

"Sure."

Mom gave me a few instructions then headed out to shovel.

Ever since basketball had started, I hadn't been thinking about much else. It seemed it took all of my energy to plan out everything with Rory so that I could play. The excitement of the games and tournaments had all of my attention. Now that I was into a routine, I realized that I had really been missing this in my life. I loved everything about basketball. I loved the way my body felt after I had worked it as hard as I could. I liked the satisfaction of figuring out what my check was going to do and stealing the ball. I liked the joking and laughing with the girls. I liked the sounds of the fans and squeak of my shoes when I made a sharp turn. I loved the energy that was created as we gathered around Coach A before the game started. I knew that I could not give it up.

I started dinner and set the table. I looked out the window. The snow was still coming down. Mom was almost done, but there was already a fresh layer of snow where she had shovelled. The walk would need to be shovelled again. I saw her stop and put her hand on her back. Then she carefully finished the last bit before coming in.

★★★

On Wednesday, we had another league game. It was a twenty-minute walk to the school where the game was being played. I would barely have enough time to run home from there to get Rory from Ming's house after the game.

The other team was a good match for us, in the first half anyway. At halftime we were tied, but we could see that the other team was not as fit as we were. By the last quarter, they just couldn't keep up with us. With about five minutes left, Coach A gave us specific goals and once again told us to hold off on the fast break. We ended up winning by fifteen points.

I was a little sad that I couldn't hang around after the game, but I didn't have much time. As always, I thought about the game on the run home. I replayed what I was proud of in my mind. I thought about what I had done wrong and what I would do better next time.

I realized that the six o'clock game would be the next week. I would just tell Mom that I wanted to watch

Hala play again and that Ming had agreed to take care of Rory. I didn't see any reason why it wouldn't work.

When I got to Ming's, Rory said, "We are almost done, Jo. Just a few minutes. We have to finish building the dragon's cave."

I looked at my phone. We had a few minutes, but not much more. I finally had to take Rory's hand and bring him toward the door. "You can finish it tomorrow," I said. "Mom's going to be home soon."

"Bye, Rory." Ming was trying to be helpful. He knew he had a sweet deal taking care of Rory and he didn't want to risk my mom finding out. "I will keep everything right here until tomorrow. Okay, buddy?"

Rory sighed. "Okay. Bye, Ming."

As Rory and I headed toward our back door I saw that the door was slightly open. Ming must not have closed it properly.

"You and Ming have to make sure you close the door, Rory," I said.

"Ming always does," Rory replied.

"But look. It's open." As I was saying it, I realized what it might mean. "Did he check it today?"

"Yes, he always checks."

I felt a chill go through me. Someone else had been in the house, maybe was still in there. I felt sick. We couldn't go in.

"I want to go back to Ming's," Rory said.

"Good idea." As we started the short walk back to

Ming's, I thought about how Mom was going to react. We were heading down the street when we heard Mom.

"Rory! Jo! Where are you going?" Mom had poked her head out the front door and was calling after us.

"Mom?" I called back. "You're home?"

With relief, Rory and I ran back to the house. I gave Mom a big hug and she hugged me back, hard.

"Where were you two? I was so worried."

I gulped. "Umm. We were just out for a walk. You know, getting some fresh air."

Mom looked confused. "A walk? You walk home from school every day and that's usually more walking than either of you want to do. What made you go out for a walk?"

"You're home early! How come?" I tried to change the subject.

"Oh, well, it's just fifteen minutes early. Our meeting was a little shorter than usual, so we got to leave."

"That's nice." I wanted to keep her talking, get her mind off of why Rory and I hadn't been at home. "I'll help with dinner, Mom. What should we make?"

And with that, we were off the topic of "the walk." Crisis averted.

That night in my room, the feeling I had when I saw the open door would not leave me. We were safe now, but I thought about how every day the house was left unlocked. I was going to have to trust Ming with a key. There was an extra key hanging in the garage that I hadn't used in years. When I first got my own house key I kept misplacing it, so Mom put an extra one in the garage. I could use the keypad garage entry to get the key if I ever forgot or lost my own. I would just give that key to Ming. I didn't need one more thing to worry about.

14 Girls' NIGHT

Thursday came and went, and soon Jenna and I were once again working on our shooting with Coach A. We did a lot of the same drills from the week before. I could already feel myself moving less awkwardly.

"Great job, girls! Have a good weekend."

"Bye, Coach," Jenna replied. "You too."

"Bye. Thank you," I added.

I was always a little disappointed at this time of the week. I missed playing basketball on Saturday and Sunday. I wished there was somewhere I could go to practice.

"Hey, you wanna come over tonight?" asked Jenna. "Hala's coming and maybe Rachel. We are going to watch a movie and make pizza."

"Yeah, that sounds fun. What time?"

"Around seven-thirty."

Jenna and Hala had already made plans. I was really happy that they were including me, but it kind of felt like I was an add-on. They were going to get together with or without me. They had already picked out a movie and Jenna's mom had taken them out to choose their pizza toppings. I shook the jealousy aside and tried to look forward to a fun evening.

Mom was happy to see me getting out. She was always telling me to get out with my friends more, but it used to just be Hala. Now that I was on the team, I was getting to know other girls, too. Mom drove me over to Jenna's and said she was going to take Rory out for a doughnut.

She watched to make sure I got in safely and she was off. I told her I would let her know when I needed to be picked up. I didn't want to arrange for her to get me too early. I didn't want to miss out on the fun the other girls would continue to have without me.

We all made our mini pizzas. Hala was a vegetarian and Jenna loved meat. Rachel chose plain cheese pizza. I liked everything, but I decided to have mushroom, bacon and tomatoes. We put our pizzas in the oven, set the timer and started watching our movie.

Jenna's basement was huge. There was a big screen TV and a soft comfy couch with a snuggly blanket for everyone. We were so cozy and comfortable that, when the timer for the pizza went off, no one wanted to get it.

"Pizzas are done!" Jenna's mom called from upstairs.

"Okay!" Jenna answered. "Be right back," she said to us.

"I'll help," Hala offered.

The movie was paused and Rachel and I were left to wait for the return of the food.

"I can't wait for the next tournament," I began. "I love when we get to play on the weekends."

"Yeah, it's fun," Rachel agreed. "But I wish my stupid brother didn't have to drive me."

"What? Why?" I asked.

"Well, lots of reasons. But mainly because he hates that he has to use his time to drive me. Then, once he's there, he thinks he is my coach. All the way home he talks about what other players did and what I did wrong."

"Oh, that must be a bad drive home," I replied.

"Like, last tournament, he kept talking about what an intense player you were. He kept asking why I couldn't get into the game a little more."

"Really?" I felt bad that Matt made Rachel feel bad. But I was flattered to be pointed out as an example of anything good in basketball.

"I mean, I like basketball and all. But I don't think I get into it the way you and Hala do. It's more about something to do with my friends and getting a bit of exercise," Rachel continued. "Oh, and then there's the way all the girls giggle and talk about my brother. It's just so creepy."

"Yeah, that must be weird," I agreed.

"It is." She paused. "Thank you for not being one of those girls. You are one of the few people I know who is more into basketball than boys," she laughed.

I laughed along with her. She was right. I mean,

I liked boys okay, just nowhere near as much as basketball. "I'm sorry you have to deal with that," I said.

"Thanks," she replied. "It's good to get it off my chest. The other girls wouldn't understand."

I felt bad for Rachel, but her confiding in me made me feel good. I started feeling guilty that I had these good feelings about the misery she shared with me.

Just then, Hala and Jenna came down, each balancing two pizzas and pop.

"That smells delicious!" Rachel cried out. "Oh, man, give me that."

Hala pulled it back.

"Okay, pretty please and thank you," Rachel said.

Hala gave the pizza to Rachel. "That's better," she laughed.

We turned the movie back on and started in on our food. It really was good. Mom and Rory and I hardly ever had pizza at home, and it was a real treat for me. The bigger treat was hanging out with the girls, though. The time went quickly.

"Oh, my brother's here," Rachel said after checking her phone. "Thanks so much for having us over, Jenna."

"It was fun. I'm so glad you could come. Oh, wait, Matt's picking you up?" Jenna smiled.

"Yes." Rachel rolled her eyes and looked at me. We shared a 'see what I mean?' look. "Do you need a ride home, Jo?"

I thought about how Mom would appreciate not having to go out in the cold. I wanted to stay with Hala and Jenna, but I decided to think about my Mom for a change. I thought about how Coach A said we sometimes needed to change our plans to benefit everyone.

"Sure, that would be great. My mom will be so happy to not have to get Rory up and drive over here." I texted Mom that I had a ride home.

"Bye," I said to Jenna and Hala.

"Thanks," Rachel said again. She waved and we headed out the door and home.

★★★

"Hi!" I called softly when I got in the back door.

"Hi, honey." Mom came over and gave me a big hug. "I feel like I have barely seen you these last few days. Did you have a fun night?"

"It was so much fun, Mom," I answered. "We made our own pizza, watched a movie, talked about bas — um, talked, laughed. I can't remember when I have had so much fun."

I could see Mom was really happy for me. One time she told me that she found it impossible to be happy if one of her children was really sad or hurt. She just absorbed the pain that Rory or I felt, and it became a part of her. Today, she shared in my joy. It felt good to see the light in her eyes.

15 RORY

I woke up with a smile on my face. I had really enjoyed my evening with the girls. I got up and wandered into the kitchen. Mom was sitting at the table reading her book. She was just putting down her coffee mug when she spotted me.

"Morning, Sunshine!" Mom teased as I let out a huge yawn. "Up late?"

I nodded and looked around the kitchen.

"Where's Rory?" I asked. It was awfully quiet for eleven o'clock on a Saturday morning.

"Oh, weirdest thing," Mom began. "Ming came over and asked if Rory wanted to go to the park." She scrunched up her face, like she just couldn't understand it. "Awfully nice of him, and Rory was super excited to go. But why would Ming want to take Rory to the park? I wonder if he has some good-deeds challenge he is trying to fulfill," she laughed.

I was a little annoyed with Ming. I didn't want him to do anything that would get Mom asking these kinds of questions. It was weird that he wanted to spend even more time with Rory. Ming and Rory must have enjoyed being together even more than I realized. I tried to forget that I could probably be paying him half as much as I was. Ming was a really nice kid, but a little different. He didn't seem to have many friends.

"That is a bit strange," I agreed. "But it probably just helps him feel useful." If only Mom knew why the bond between Ming and Rory had grown so strong . . .

"Maybe." Mom paused for a moment. "What are you up to today?"

"I have a bit of homework. Then I just want to relax, watch some TV," I answered.

"Oh, I saw a new movie on Netflix, kind of a chick flick. Do you want to watch it with me after Rory is in bed tonight?"

"Sure," I nodded. It had been a while since Mom and I had spent time together, just the two of us. I missed that. I missed being her little girl. "That would be really nice." I went behind Mom's chair and reached my arms around her, snuggling my face in her neck.

A wave of guilt washed over me. Mom trusted me. I was deceiving her. If I wanted to keep playing basketball, I had to tell her. But I just couldn't make myself take the chance, not yet. I would wait until the season was over. I couldn't bear the thought of not seeing it through to the end.

That night we watched the movie together and the rest of the weekend passed quickly.

On Monday morning, my alarm went off, yanking me from a pretty great dream about shooting the winning basket in the finals. I hit the snooze button and willed my way back into the dream. I was standing on the free-throw line with three seconds left in the game. I sank the first foul shot. The score changed to 55–55. I looked at the basket and prepared myself for the final shot, just as my alarm sounded again. I slammed it off and sighed.

"Ugggh . . ." I rolled myself out of bed and started getting ready for the day.

I peeked outside and could see the sun was shining. Spring was on its way. I couldn't wait. I didn't really mind winter that much, but I was really ready for it to be done. I just wanted to slide into my flip-flops and run out the door with no coat or sweater.

I got dressed and wandered into the kitchen. Mom had already left for work. I woke Rory and told him to get dressed. I started getting our lunches together and making breakfast.

Rory shuffled into the kitchen with his T-shirt on backward and his hair sticking up everywhere. I had to laugh. I took my phone out to snap a quick photo and sent it to Mom, hoping it would make her smile. She and I had had a nice time on the weekend. I wanted to keep that feeling going.

This is what you are missing. I clicked send.

LOL, she replied.

Rory and I ate a little breakfast, grabbed our backpacks and headed to school.

"Ming took me to the park," he announced as we walked along the sidewalk. "He helped me do the monkey bars. I almost did the whole way across. I am strong. Ming said so. He said he couldn't do the monkey bars until grade three. He says I am amazing." Rory puffed out his chest a little as he said this.

"You are amazing, Rory," I said.

He turned and looked at me. I saw his big round eyes full of sadness. "My teacher doesn't think I am amazing. She thinks I am stupid."

"What are you talking about? No, she doesn't. Why would you say that?" I stiffened up and felt a knot growing in the pit of my stomach.

"Ms. Short sends me out with Mrs. B and Porter, and Porter doesn't even know the alphabet. Ms. B teaches us the letters. I know the letters. I told Ms. Short I know all the letters. She said she knows that, but she wants me to work with Porter and Ms. B anyway. She doesn't believe me. She thinks I don't know anything."

"Maybe Ms. Short thinks you're a good helper."

"Ms. B is his helper. I am not his helper."

We walked the rest of the way in silence. I felt bad for Rory. I knew how he felt. He wanted to prove himself, show what he knew. He didn't think he was getting a fair chance. Rory was a different kid, but he was smart. He just wasn't great with people. It was hard for him to make friends, and he had difficulty with his emotions. He cried easily and had frequent outbursts when he was upset. I did notice that, since he had been hanging around with Ming, there had been very few problems.

"Bye, Rory," I said as we got to the school. "I will come get you this afternoon. Have a great day! Don't worry. I am sure your teacher knows you are smart. She just thinks you are a good helper." I gave him a hug before heading down to the far end of the building, where Hala and Rachel were laughing about something.

We walked inside together, and soon we were talking about basketball. The playoffs were coming up and we were expected to do well in our division. Maybe we could even win and qualify for the provincial championship. Soon the final bell for the start of class sounded and we went off to homeroom.

16 BUSTED

After school, I rushed to get Rory. Then I remembered how unhappy he had been that morning.

"Excuse me, Ms. Short?" I said to Rory's teacher.

"Oh, hi, Jo. How are you?" Ms. Short knew all of her students' siblings by name. If she met you once, she would not forget you.

"I just wanted to ask you something quickly."

She put down the pen she had in her hand. "Of course. What is it?"

"Well, Rory was really upset this morning, because he is feeling like you don't think he is smart," I started. She looked at me like she needed a little more to work with. "I guess he has been going out to get extra work on his letters? He knows them all, so . . ."

"Oh, dear," she said. "I am so sorry he thinks that. I know Rory is a bright boy, but he is one of the few kids who can work with Porter. Porter has really taken a liking to him, you know, and doesn't have any friends in class. I was just hoping that going out together might help Porter connect to someone. I feel terrible that Rory doesn't know how clever I think he is." She paused. "Rory does have his challenges too, as far as friendships go. I just thought the two of them might hit it off. I will think about how I can clear this up with Rory."

I looked at the clock and knew I had to get going if I had any hope of being back for practice. "Uh, okay, thanks, Ms. Short. I better get going."

Rory was waiting for me just outside the school doors. I grabbed him and we hurried home. The whole way I was thinking, Rory doesn't have friends? I felt terrible. I realized that he never got invited to play with a friend and never talked about his friends at school. I couldn't remember the last time he had been invited to a birthday party. I guess I had known for some time that he struggled, but I just hadn't really thought about it for a while. It was starting to make even more sense to me why he enjoyed going to Ming's so much. Why he never complained about rushing home and spending time with Ming.

We arrived home ten minutes later than usual. I rushed out the door and ran full speed. I had five minutes to get to practice.

When I ran into the gym, I could see all the girls gathered around Coach A. I quickly changed and joined in the drill they were already doing. I knew Coach A saw me, but she didn't say anything. I didn't question why, but quietly thanked the powers that be for her silence.

She worked us hard and practice went a little overtime. Everyone slumped into the change room after we finished, dead tired. I had no time to rest, just grabbed my stuff and headed out.

"Jo!" I heard Coach A calling after me. But I pretended not to hear and ran off. I had no time to waste. I couldn't afford to get started on a conversation that would take more than ten seconds.

As I ran home, I found myself thinking about Rory again. I thought Rory was a great kid. He had his oddities, like any kid, but he was nice enough. I arrived at Ming's with only a few minutes to spare.

"C'mon, Rory," I said. "We're late. We have to hurry."

He acted like he didn't hear me and kept on moving his Lego figures here and there.

"Rory!" I yelled. "We have to go!"

My whole body felt wound up, like I was going to explode and fly into a thousand tiny pieces if I had to deal with one more thing. I just couldn't keep this up anymore. I knew if I didn't come clean with Mom I was going to crack. I felt my eyes stinging.

Rory and Ming both looked at me with wide eyes and their mouths hanging open.

Then Rory got up and headed to the door to put on his jacket and boots. I bent down to roughly push his boots on and quickly tied the laces. He fumbled with his jacket and I grabbed his hand. Rory looked back over his shoulder at Ming as I pulled him out the door without saying good-bye.

Rory and I walked home in silence. Mom pulled into the driveway just as Rory and I were putting our jackets away. I turned on the TV and tried to look relaxed, as though we had been sitting there for hours.

"Hi, there," Mom said. She came over and kissed each of our heads from behind the couch. "How was everyone's day?"

"Okay," I said.

Mom came around to the front of the couch and looked at me, then at Rory.

"What's going on?" she asked.

"Why? What do you mean?" I answered.

"I don't know. You both seem kind of distant."

"Just tired, Mom," I said. It wasn't a lie.

"Okay, if you say so." She didn't seem convinced. But I could tell she was tired too and just didn't have the energy to get into it.

I helped Mom with dinner. All three of us were pretty quiet and went off to do our own things when we were done.

Hey. I read the text from Hala as I was lying on my bed. I couldn't seem to make myself do anything. Coach was looking for you after practice.

Really? I texted back. What did she want?

The phone in the kitchen was ringing and no one was answering. We hardly ever answered the phone anymore if we didn't recognize the number. It always seemed to be some scammer or solicitor. We hated trying to get rid of them once we answered the phone. It was easier to just let the person leave a message and we would call back if needed. I heard the answering machine kick in as I looked at Hala's response.

Not sure. I just heard her calling after you when you left. I thought you must have heard her, but I guess you were too far away already

I couldn't tell her that I actually heard Coach A. I didn't have the energy for that conversation.

I guess so. I wonder what she wanted. As I sent the text, I heard a familiar voice on the answering machine. It was hard to hear the message from my room, but there was no mistaking the voice. It was Coach A.

Gotta go. TTYL, I texted Hala and ran into the kitchen.

The message was ending just as I got there. What did Coach A want? Why was she calling the house? I couldn't let Mom hear the message. The wheels in my brain were turning, trying to remember which button to push to erase the message without playing it. I would find out tomorrow what she wanted.

I was bending down to peer at the buttons on the answering machine when I heard Mom come in from behind me.

"Did you hear who called?" she asked.

"Oh, some scam, I think."

"Well, play it. Let's see what the scam of the day is."

She shook her head in disgust and, before I knew it, she had pressed play. There was Coach A's voice, loud and clear, coming through the phone speaker.

"Hi, Ms. Beck, this is Coach A calling, Jo's basketball coach. I was hoping you had a few minutes to chat about some possible summer camps for Jo. She has really improved since the start of the season and I know she would like to keep working on her skills over the summer. Give me a call back when you get a chance. I just received a bunch of the summer camp brochures. I was going to send them today with Jo, but she left practice before I could get them to her." She left some contact information, then hung up.

I cannot even describe the look on Mom's face when she looked at me. All she said was, "Joanna Beck, I think you have some explaining to do."

17 Breaking POINT

"I know, Mom," I began. "I've been wanting to tell you for a long time, but I was just so afraid you wouldn't let me play." And then the tears came. All the pent-up guilt, worry and anxiety burst forth and I didn't even try to talk. I couldn't. Mom waited patiently for several minutes, then she got serious.

"Okay, Jo. That's enough. What is this all about?"

I told her everything. It just came tumbling out of my mouth. She didn't interrupt me. She just let me spill my guts until she had heard it all. Then she put her head in her hands. When she looked up, I could see her eyes were moist. She took my hands in hers and looked at me before she began.

"Jo, you know I have always trusted you." Now it was her turn to talk. I just sat there and listened. "We have always been open and honest with each other. I would be lying if I said I wasn't disappointed that you felt you couldn't come to me. And you're probably right. I probably would not have let you play. Your first responsibility is to our family. I have always taught you that. I have had troubles with Rory's care in the past, and I just need you to help out for a little longer."

The disappointment she felt in my actions hurt, but it was nothing compared to the pain I was feeling at the thought of giving up basketball. I wasn't sure anyone could understand what playing basketball had brought into my life. It was in my blood. My reason to get up in the morning.

Mom paused and took a deep breath. Then she slowly let it out.

"Jo," she said, "you found a good solution on your own. But you were deceptive. That's what I'm having trouble with right now."

"I know, Mom. I'm sorry. I wanted to tell you, but I wanted to play more." I put my head down in shame and felt a few more tears trickle warmly down my cheeks. I wiped them away with the back of my hand. I should have told Mom. I knew that, but I didn't regret what I had done. It had opened up a whole new world to me. "Mom, I will do anything to make this up to you. But the playoffs are coming up and I — I just . . ." I started crying again and couldn't stop. "I . . . I . . ." I sniffled. "I just want to play."

Mom sighed again. "I need some time to think, Jo. But for tomorrow you will be here after school to take care of Rory. We will talk after I get home from work."

My worst fears had come true and I had no idea how to handle it.

I couldn't sleep that night. I couldn't stand not knowing what was going to happen. I couldn't handle the thought of not playing. I wanted to talk to someone about it, but I had closed everyone off from my little secret. Even my best friend had no idea what I had been doing. There was no one to talk to.

What would I do if Mom wouldn't let me finish the season? I couldn't bear thinking about it.

My mind drifted in and out of different things. I thought about Rory and how sad I felt for him. I thought about Mom and how disappointed she was in me. I thought about Ming and how much the time with Rory meant to him. I thought about Hala and how hurt she would be that I didn't share my secret with her. I thought about how Coach A would react when I told her I wouldn't be able to play anymore.

I wanted to scream. I wanted to bang and pound on the walls. Instead, I kicked my desk, then grabbed my toe in pain and started to cry again.

After a couple of hours, I found myself lacing on my runners and throwing on a light jacket. I walked out the front door and closed it behind me. It hadn't snowed for a while and the sidewalks and streets were clear, though the snow still covered the ground. I started to run, faster and faster. My steps created a rhythm. Soon words were bouncing in my head to match the pounding beat of my shoes on the ground.

O-ver, o-ver, everything is o-ver. O-ver, o-ver, everything is o-ver. O-ver, o-ver, everything is o-ver. Like a song bug in my ear, it wouldn't leave, just repeated again and again. I kept running, farther and farther, faster and faster, trying to escape my thoughts. I was getting warm and I felt sweat starting to drip down my face and into my eyes. Still I ran, on and on.

I didn't know how much time passed before I started to feel tired, my legs heavy. Soon I found myself just sitting in the snow. I heard my breath begin to slow down, as if I was listening to myself from outside my body. I was suddenly really tired. I didn't know how I would make it back home. What would Mom do if I didn't come home, if I got hurt and was brought to the hospital? Maybe she would feel guilty for not being more understanding. The thought comforted me briefly. But then I started to think of how tired Mom always was, how worried she'd be. It no longer made me feel good. My love for basketball had turned me into a horrible person.

I don't know how long I sat there, but it was long enough that the heat from my run wore off and I began to shiver. I stood up and began plodding in the direction of home. I realized I did not have my phone or any money with me. I had just one way to get home. I walked slowly, hands in my jacket pockets, head down.

By the time I got back, it was really late. I walked up the steps to the front door and turned the knob.

Locked.

Of course. Mom didn't even know I was gone. She had left me in my room to think and had locked up the house for the night before going to bed. I tried the back door and was not surprised to find that it was also locked. I sighed heavily. I knew we had a spare key in the garage. I walked down the sidewalk to the garage behind the house, punched in the code and stepped inside. I turned on the light and reached for the hook that held the spare key. My hand stopped in mid-air as I saw the empty hook. I had given that key to Ming.

I was exhausted, mentally and physically. I grabbed a ratty old blanket from a shelf in the garage and curled up in a corner to sleep.

18 Moment of TRUTH

I woke a few hours later to the sound of the recycling truck as it clanged down the back lane. Where was I? Then the events of the night before came flooding back.

A few minutes later, I heard the back door open, and then the back gate. Soon I heard the wheels of the recycling bin rolling toward me. The code to the garage was being punched in. I jumped to my feet and ran to the side door of the garage. I opened it and ran outside just as Mom opened the overhead door by the back lane. She was returning the recycling bin to the inside of the garage. I slowly crept into the back door of the house just in time to see Mom coming back.

I was so cold I could barely stand. I hopped into the shower and felt the warm water flow over me. I heard Mom open the bathroom door to say, "I will be home early today. We'll talk more." Then she left. She had no idea that I had even been gone. I felt more alone than ever.

When I had finally warmed up, I forced myself to get

out of the shower. I helped Rory get ready for school.

Rory and I walked in silence, slower than usual. I was not planning to go to school. I just couldn't face everything that I had to deal with. I needed more time to think. I couldn't face Coach A or Hala before knowing exactly what my punishment would be. Mostly I could not sit in class all day, unable to focus on a single thing.

I said good-bye to Rory and headed back home.

I got into bed and pulled the covers up over me. It felt good to be warm. I had had only a few hours of sleep. The lack of rest was taking its toll and, before I knew it, I was fast asleep.

The ping of my phone woke me up. When I finally looked at it, I realized that I had slept through countless pings. Messages flooded my screen, mostly from Hala. The lone one from Mom stood out and I opened the message.

It was simply a heart emoji.

I started looking through the messages from Hala.

Coach gave me some summer camp brochures. Do you want to go together? That was from last night before I had left the house. Then about an hour later, **Jo? Hello?** About an hour after that: **I want to go to the one at the U of W the first week in August. It would be so much fun. Text me.**

Early in the morning she had sent, **Talk 2 u at school.** Then after school had started, **Where R U?!!!!**

I texted her back. Not feeling well.

She responded right away. OMG I was so worried. Playoffs this weekend, hope u feel better soon. Go to the doctor, plz!!!

I sent a smiley face.

I just didn't have the energy for anything more, so I set my phone back down on my nightstand. I started thinking about how my conversation with Mom would go. She was disappointed in me. Why hadn't I just told her? But I knew why. If there was even a one per cent chance that she wouldn't let me play, it was too big a risk for me to take. But now I had ruined it all.

I tried to distract myself with stupid TV shows on Netflix. Eventually, it was time to go get Rory, so I threw on my jacket and walked to school. I gave myself plenty of time because I had no interest in moving quickly. My body was so heavy it felt like it was made out of lead. When I got to the school, I waited in my usual spot for Rory. He came out right away, running toward me.

"I was a helper today!" He beamed up at me proudly.

"That's great, Rory," I replied listlessly. Then I remembered how sad Rory had been the other day when he thought his teacher thought he was dumb. "What did you help with?"

"I got to write on the big chart paper during the 'we do it together' part of writing. Ms. Short said she liked how I remembered to use upper case letters for the names of people and to start the sentences."

"That's really great, Rory," I said, and I meant it. It put a small light back in me to see his eyes light up when he talked. "I knew Ms. Short thought you were smart."

Rory continued to walk proudly and turned to me with a big smile. There was a bounce in his step. I found myself walking more quickly than I had been in order to keep up with him.

Shortly after we arrived home, Mom pulled into the driveway. I took a deep breath. The moment of truth was upon me.

19 COMMITMENT

"Hello?" Mom called in the door. She was home a lot earlier than usual.

Rory looked at me, clearly confused. Out the front window we could both see Ming walking up the sidewalk. He got to the back door just as Mom was entering the kitchen.

"Hello," Mom said. "How are you, Ming?"

"Ah . . . good," he responded. He looked over to me and Rory with a big question mark on his face.

"Hi, Ming!" Rory ran to the back door. "I was a helper today!"

"Wow! Good for you, buddy," Ming said with a big smile on his face.

"You were?" Mom said. "How exciting!" She paused. "I guess you will be taking Rory for a bit?"

Ming looked terrified. He knew Mom was not supposed to know about our arrangement and that it would probably end if she ever found out. I could tell he was struggling over how to answer.

"Yeah, Ming," I told him. "That would be great. Mom and I need to talk." We gave each other knowing looks. He understood that Mom had somehow found out something. How much, he didn't know. He was a smart kid. He knew not to say too much and give away something Mom might not yet know about.

"Okay, let's go, buddy." He turned to Rory.

The two of them headed off to Ming's. Mom and I stared at each other.

"Just let me change out of my work clothes, Jo," she said. "Then we need to have a long talk."

When Mom came back we sat down in the kitchen. She made us both some tea, then she started talking.

"I called your coach," she said.

I snapped my head up. "What?" Of all the things I had imagined happening, Mom talking to my coach did not enter my mind. I was embarrassed. Now Coach A knew about my secrets and lies.

"I called the number Coach A left on the answering machine," Mom continued. "We had a long talk."

I put my head back, closed my eyes and let out a groan.

"Quite the tangled web you have woven," she said. "I understand that I signed some papers and paid some basketball fees?"

I nodded my head and smiled weakly. "I'm sorry, Mom," I said. And then I felt guilty again. I was lying. I wasn't sorry. If I had the chance, I would probably do it all again. I had to be honest now. There was something I was sorry about. "I'm sorry that I hurt you and ruined the trust you have in me. But I had to do it, Mom." I paused. "I knew you wouldn't let me play."

Mom sighed. "You're right."

We sat in silence for a while.

"Now what?" I asked.

Mom took another deep breath. "I have been doing a lot of thinking since last night, Jo. I have come to realize that maybe I have been unfair to you. I started thinking back to when I was your age and how desperately I wanted to have a group of friends. But I always had to go home to help with the family store. It was expected, and it was needed. My mom and dad had to work hard to keep the store going and they could not afford to pay for extra help. We all worked together and I didn't question it. When I needed your help, I didn't question it either. I just expected you to do your part."

I waited.

"Coach A really cares about you and the team," she continued. "She was very upset that I knew nothing about you playing."

I felt sick. Coach A was one of the best people I knew. My actions had made her feel bad. What kind of person was I? My selfishness hit me like a ton of bricks. How could I ever face her again?

"You know how I feel about commitment, Jo.

You have started something here. Maybe dishonestly, but that is not Coach A's fault and it is not your teammates' fault."

"I know." I hung my head.

"You will finish the season and play in the playoffs."

My head popped up. "What?" Did I understand her correctly? I was going to play?

"Yes," she went on. "Your coach and your teammates have come to count on you. If I punish you, I will also be punishing them. And I simply cannot do that."

I felt the life coming back into my body. "Mom, thank you." I wiped away the tears, happy ones at last. "I will make it up to you. I promise."

"You made a very smart arrangement with Ming. I can see that it has been very good for Rory." She paused and took a deep breath. "And now I must apologize, Jo. I can see how my expectations of you have kept you from making friends and doing things you love. A thirteen-year-old girl should be able to go out and have fun sometimes."

I could not believe what I was hearing. How could this be happening?

"Coach A says you work really hard," Mom continued. "She says your passion creates a great energy for the team."

She held up some brochures for summer basketball camp. "I stopped by the school to pick these up on my way home."

"I can go?" I asked hopefully.

"We'll see. Let's take a look at the brochures together and see what we can work out. Maybe Ming would like a summer job taking care of Rory during the time you are at camp."

I couldn't believe it. Playing the rest of the season. And maybe going to basketball camp. "Mom, I will never forget this. Thank you, thank you, thank you." I flung myself at her and hugged her long and hard before letting go.

"Okay, then." Mom put the brochures on the table. "Now, we have one more thing to discuss. As I see it, there are about one hundred hours over the last few months that I trusted you to be with Rory. You did make sure he was safe and cared for, but that is still one hundred hours of lies and deceit that you will pay back in some way with honest work. I have all kinds of ideas." Mom smiled. She reached for a chart she had already made to track my hours.

I nodded. I wanted to prove myself and earn back Mom's trust. We had reached an understanding, a better understanding than I ever thought possible.

20 Let's Do THIS

I was going to play. I couldn't wait to tell Hala the great news.

Then I stopped myself. Hala did not know about what I had been going through. She didn't know that I had been thinking I was going to have to quit. By not sharing what was going on in my life with Hala, I had robbed myself of having someone to share my joy with. I felt a pang in my chest. What had Coach A said? Something about the cost of poor choices? I was now paying for my choices.

I picked up my phone. No messages.

Hala would still be at practice, but I had to text something. **Feeling better, see u tmrw.**

A while later I went over to Ming's place to get Rory. Mom had said that having Ming take care of Rory was a good idea. I felt proud of myself. It was a good idea. It was costing me all my savings, but I could see how much Rory loved having someone to play with. Ming seemed happier too, even joking now and then. It was a side of him I had not seen a couple of months ago.

Ming invited me in and asked what was going on. "Your mom knows? What's going to happen? You said if she found out this would be over."

"That's what I thought," I said. "But Mom and I worked it out. She thinks you're good for Rory."

"Really?" He smiled the same way Rory had when he said his teacher was proud of him. I guessed that everyone needed to feel needed. Everyone needed to be a part of something beyond themselves. Basketball had done this for me.

I smiled back. "Really," I said.

"Sooooo . . . I am going to keep babysitting Rory?"

"Yes."

I could see the relief he felt. I didn't know if it was the friendship, the being needed or the money. Maybe it was all three.

Mom was getting dinner ready when we got back. I helped set the table. I would do everything I could to show Mom that I was grateful. We ate together and I offered to clean up.

"Let's do it together," Mom said.

We cleared the table and put away the extra food. Mom washed the pots and I dried. We didn't say much, but I felt close to her. The wall was gone.

As we were putting the last dishes away, she said, "Jo, I want to encourage you to come to me with things and be honest with me. I don't want any more sneaking around and lies." She paused. "I realize that I have to listen to you and be reasonable if I want that to happen. You have probably used almost all of your hard-earned money to pay Ming, so I have to assume that basketball is worth it."

"It is worth it, Mom. I don't ever feel more like myself than when I am playing basketball."

"Well," said Mom, "then I am happy you found your passion. Some people spend a long time trying to find something to get fired up about."

"Mom," I said when we were all done. "I just want you to know how much this means to me. Thank you for letting me play. Will you come and watch the playoffs?"

"Well, I am curious about this passion Coach A talked about," she laughed. "So I guess I'll have to come and see for myself."

I knew I needed to do one more thing before playoffs. Hala's friendship was important to me. More than anything, I wanted to share what I had been going through with her. Over and over again she had checked up on me. She cared about me and I had lied. That night, I picked up my phone and called her.

"Hi, Jo. What's up?" she asked.

"Do you have a few minutes?"

"Of course. Is everything okay?" Once again, Hala was worried about me.

"Yes, it is now."

Then I did what I should have done months ago. I told her why I had been rushing out after practice. I told her about all the times I had been "sick." I told her everything. She listened.

"Wow," she said when I was done.

"I know. I am so sorry, Hala. I made a lot of really bad decisions. I messed up. I want you to know how much I appreciate you. I hope you can forgive me."

Hala admitted that she was hurt. She wondered why I had not trusted her. We talked for a long time. In the end, Hala understood. She forgave me. Sharing my secrets had made our friendship stronger. I knew that we could get through anything together. There would be no more lies, just truth and trust.

★★★

The week passed in a frenzy of practices as the team prepared for playoffs.

Finally, the first rounds of playoffs began. Our first games were against the teams that had not done very well. We won easily. Those games just felt the same as the league games always felt. But when we made it to the finals, everything changed.

The game was on a Saturday. It was going to be the first game Mom could come and watch. I could tell she was excited to see me play. I was excited for her to see what I had been up to for the last few months.

The finals were held in the high school gym, with real pull-out bleachers, not just chairs lining the perimeter of the junior high gym. The gym was twice the size of ours, and we would have to cover a lot more space. I was more thankful than ever for the fitness level Coach A had pushed us to achieve. And with my running back and forth to practice every day, I was more than ready.

By the time we started our warm-up the stands were filling up. When warm-up was done, there must have been a hundred people.

I was tingling with excitement.

I had never felt better. I had learned some hard lessons, but I felt stronger because of it. Mom and Rory were in the stands, waiting for the game to begin. Rory was already clapping and cheering. On one side of him sat Mom, and on the other, Ming arrived and settled in beside him.

I smiled at the way Rory's face lit up when he saw Ming. He was the big brother Rory never had.

The ref blew the whistle for one minute until game time. We huddled around Coach A.

"I believe in you girls," she began. "No matter what happens out there, we have done amazing things together, on and off the court." She looked at me, then around the whole group. "You have worked hard all season and you are ready. Let's do this!" Coach A reached her hand into the middle of the huddle and the rest of us followed.

"Three, two, one!" Hala counted down for us.

"Teamwork!" We all cheered together as we lifted our hands out of the huddle.

I headed out onto the court with Hala.

We looked at each other. "Game on," she smiled with a twinkle in her eye.

"Game on," I nodded.

The ref threw the jump ball and all my favourite sounds filled the air. This time my family was here to share the experience. I was finally home.

ACKNOWLEDGEMENTS

Thank you to Lorimer Publishing for accepting my manuscript and supporting my first publication. Special thanks to Kat Mototsune for her patience in guiding me through this process. To my husband, Michael, your ongoing encouragement and inflated belief in me as a writer means so much. To my daughter, Sydney, who is always the first to read my stories, thank you.